ORCA
YOUNG
READERS

Things are Looking Grimm, Jill

Dan Bar-el

ORCA BOOK PUBLISHERS

Library and Archives Canada Cataloguing in Publication

Bar-el, Dan
Things are looking Grimm, Jill / Dan Bar-el.
(Orca young readers)

ISBN 1-55143-400-8

I. Title. II. Series.

PS8553.A76229T43 2006   jC813'.54   C2006-901019-6

First Published in the United States 2006
Library of Congress Control Number: 2006922289

Summary: When Princess Jill receives an urgent message from a mysterious stranger, she rides off alone to rescue the women of Grimm from an evil spell.

Free teachers' guide available. www.orcabook.com

Orca Book Publishers gratefully acknowledges the support for its publishing programs provided by the following agencies: the Government of Canada through the Book Publishing Industry Development Program (BPIDP), the Canada Council for the Arts, and the British Columbia Arts Council.

Typesetting and cover design by Lynn O'Rourke
Cover & interior illustrations by Kathy Boake

In Canada:
Orca Book Publishers
www.orcabook.com
Box 5626 Stn B
Victoria, BC Canada
V8R 6S4

In the United States:
Orca Book Publishers
www.orcabook.com
PO Box 468
Custer, WA USA
98240-0468

09 08 07 06 • 6 5 4 3 2 1
Printed and bound in Canada
Printed on 100% recycled paper.
Processed chlorine-free using vegetable based inks.

For Emma and Madeleine,
two up-and-coming princesses.

To MARTIN

who supported my first book
with deeds as well as words

A good friend indeed

love,
Dan

Jack came tumbling after Jill, and that was when things started to go all wrong... again. Allow me to explain.

Princess Jill, sister of King Jack and daughter of Mother Goose, went up a hill to fetch a pail of water. She did it to prove she wasn't a spoiled princess, because if anyone had a reputation for being spoiled, it was Jill. She was so spoiled that people called her Sour Milk Jill behind her back.

You might ask why a princess need bother with doing chores, anyway, and that would be a worthy question. Aside from being an amazingly spoiled princess, Jill was quite excellent at jousting, fencing, archery, crossbow, longbow, spear throwing, running, climbing, jumping, swimming, skating and long-distance spitting. Sir Humpty Dumpty, the head of the Royal Guard, believed Jill to be a brave and plucky young woman who would stare danger right in the face even if it meant standing on a wobbly chair to do so. And so, Jill was now a Royal Guard-in-training.

But Sir Dumpty also believed that a Royal Guard had to be more than just brave and talented. A Royal Guard had to be courteous, gallant and humble as well. That is why he felt that Jill should perform some community service as a way of getting her off her high horse.

Therefore it was important that she march up the hill, pail in hand, ready to bring water to families in the kingdom who were unable to get it themselves. End of argument. Her brother, who was not in the least bit spoiled, trailed along just to make sure she didn't order someone else to do her chores for her. Jack didn't

2

think his sister would fetch water even if her bed were on fire.

Up the hill Jill went to fetch the water. So far so good. But as she filled the pail, Princess Jill noticed a horse and rider far off in the distance coming toward her at an astonishing speed. The horse sailed over every tall hedge that stood before it and the rider stayed confidently mounted.

That in itself was not strange, but as the horse and rider came closer, Jill began to feel dizzier and dizzier. As the horse came close enough for Jill to touch, she became so dizzy that she lost her balance and fell down. Her brother, not expecting this sudden change in plan, tripped over Jill and found himself also falling down the hill. Or to be truly honest, he bounced down the hill like a lopsided rock. Thus Jack came tumbling after Jill.

"Just once, I would like to walk down that hill," said Jack as he inspected his newly dented crown.

Jill picked herself up off the ground in a flash, frantically rubbing her eyes and blinking. She looked ahead and she looked behind, but the horse and rider were nowhere to be seen. "D-d-did you see that?" she asked her brother.

"See what?" Jack replied.

"Why, that white stallion with the handsome young rider, of course!" Jill yelled.

"Handsome young rider?" repeated Jack, with a snicker.

Jill clamped a hand over her mouth and blushed. She had never used the word "handsome" before in her life. Jill liked horses, it was true, but horse *riders* could look like squids with pineapples on their heads for all she cared.

And what was worse, she suddenly remembered what she was thinking as the horse and rider came closer. Jill had imagined him scooping her up with one hand and placing her gracefully onto the back of his horse as they rode into the sunset with beautiful music playing in the background and flower petals falling in their path. "Yuck!" she shouted.

"Jill, what are you going on about?" Jack stared warily at his sister.

It was obvious to Jill that her brother hadn't seen any of it, nor was it likely that he would believe her if she explained. He would probably tease her for acting like a ninny. Jill, herself, thought she was acting like a ninny. Handsome horse rider indeed, she scoffed.

"You know who could really use some water?" asked Jill innocently, changing the subject as she leaned over and picked up the pail.

This question caught Jack off guard. It was already decided that Jill would get water for the old lady who lived in a shoe. After all, the woman had way too many children and her footwear lacked decent plumbing.

"I don't know, Jill," replied Jack suspiciously. "Who?"

"Why, Miss Bo Peep! I hear she's very busy with her sheep these days. Imagine how grateful she would be for a drink of cool spring water."

"Poor Miss Bo Peep!" he gasped, fondly remembering her golden hair and sunshine smile. "Why, I wouldn't be much of a king if I left such a valued royal subject to die of thirst. I'd better hurry!"

Jill was feeling much better now. With one well-timed question, she had managed to distract her brother and get him to go back up the hill to fill the pail with water himself. At this rate, Jill thought, she might be able to become a Royal Guard and not have to do one lousy chore. Her smile became even bigger as she watched her brother drag the heavy pail toward Miss Bo Peep's farm.

In the center of Mother Goose's kingdom was the royal forest. Some forests are dark and dangerous, with fearsome animals lurking behind every tree. But this forest had lovely cobblestone paths. Some forests are shrouded in shadows where crooked old crones wait to lure you into vats of boiling oil. But this forest had beds of bright festive flowers. And there were also large plastic-bag dispensers so dragons could clean up after themselves.

Jill walked along one of the forest paths toward the castle. She was still preoccupied with the strange vision she'd had back on the hill.

"Was it a daydream?" she thought to herself. "It didn't feel like a dream. Maybe I'm coming down with the flu." Jill touched her forehead to see if she had a fever. No such luck.

As Jill turned the corner, she caught a glimpse of a dark hooded figure following her along the edge of the path. A shiver ran up Jill's spine.

Hooded figures are rarely happy sights, especially when you're all alone in a forest. First of all, hooded figures by their nature tend to keep their faces hidden. That is if they actually *have* faces. Secondly, hooded figures tend to carry tall sticks with very scary-looking blades attached to them. This does not add to their charm one iota.

However, when this hooded figure moved out of the woods, Jill could see that it carried a picnic basket, not a weapon.

Jill was also relieved to find that this hooded figure had a face. It was the face of a small girl, perhaps a year younger than Jill. The expression on this face was one of complete astonishment.

"Are you all right?" asked Jill.

The small girl didn't say anything. She was completely absorbed in looking at the woods around her.

"Hello? Is something wrong?" asked Jill.

"Oh my!" gushed the little girl. "What big trees you have!"

"Excuse me?"

"We don't have such big trees where I come from."

"You're not from around here?"

"No," replied the little girl, "I come from the land of Grimm."

"I see," said Jill. "What brings you to Mother Goose's kingdom?"

The little girl's eyes grew large with excitement. "I'm here on a mission," she whispered, giggling absurdly.

"How interesting," remarked Jill, not really meaning it. The hooded little girl was already starting to irritate the princess a lot.

"My name is Little Red Riding Hood. They call me that on account of my riding hood being red, you see. If my riding hood were blue, they would probably call me Little Blue Riding Hood. It's all very, *very* complicated."

Jill began grinding her teeth.

"I'm supposed to deliver a note to Princess Jill," Little Red Riding Hood continued. "Would you happen to know how I could find her?"

"You're looking at her, Red," said Jill.

"Oh," replied the little hooded girl glumly. "Well, that was an easy mission."

Little Red Riding Hood reached into her picnic basket and pulled out an envelope, which she handed to Jill. It said: *For Princess Jill's Eyes Only. Urgent!* Jill opened the envelope and unfolded the paper within. This is what was written:

My dearest Princess Jill,
If you are reading this, and your mind remains un-tampered-with, then all is not yet lost!

Something horrible has befallen the land of Grimm. Some strange spell has taken hold of all our women, but the menfolk are blind to all of it. The worst of it is happening in the regions near Prince Charming's castle. I am powerless to protect anyone against it or to put a stop to it myself.

I know about you, Jill. Over the years, I've become aware of your reputation. I believe that you have the strength to overcome this vile magic and restore the land of Grimm to its original harmony. If you do come, be careful! I think they already know that you are being contacted.

Yours in gratitude,
F.G.

P.S. Sorry about the messenger. She was all I could scrounge up.

"Who gave you this note?" asked Jill.

"Some lady in a sparkly dress. I don't know her. But she said she would introduce me to Prince Charming if I did this errand. Oh, the prince! I am so in love with him. SO IN LOVE WITH HIM! I'm going to marry him one day and live happily ever after."

Little Red Riding Hood said this with the most insane look on her face. Jill remembered how the letter began with concern that her mind hadn't been tampered with. Had Little Red Riding Hood's mind been tampered with? Or was she just, you know, annoying?

Jill didn't have a chance to find out, because Little Red Riding Hood turned on her heel and headed back into the forest.

"Wait a second!" shouted Jill.

It was no use. Little Red Riding Hood was long gone, although Jill could still hear her singing, "I'm going to marry Prince Charming. I'm going to marry Prince Charming."

Jill looked down at the letter. Perhaps if an odd little girl handed you a note from a mysterious stranger asking you to leave your home in order to save a distant land, you might take a day or two to consider it. I, myself, would have buried my head in the ground like an ostrich until the odd little girl got bored and went away.

But Jill was not like that. Jill was always up for an adventure. Life was generally too slow for her. She didn't like chores, but she wasn't put off by the possibility of danger.

"Just who is this F.G.?" Jill asked herself. "How come she knows all about me?" Not that it mattered, because Jill decided to go anyway. It was too intriguing to resist.

But first she ran off to the castle to see her mother.

Princess Jill found Mother Goose standing in the middle of the castle's great hall, staring up at the clock with her arms crossed. Reginald, the castle butler, stood behind Jill's mother in the exact same pose. Both were tapping their feet impatiently.

"You're late, Jillian!" snapped Mother Goose as soon as Jill stuck her head through the door. "Dance lessons were to begin twenty minutes ago!"

"Oh," groaned Jill, remembering her appointment. Jill and her brother Jack endured weekly instruction in ballroom dancing. It was not a choice; it was a royal command.

"And where's your brother?" Mother Goose snapped again.

Jill immediately regretted having talked Jack into taking water to Bo Peep. Now she would have to face the music, so to speak, all by herself.

"Jack's...kind of busy, Mother," replied Jill reluctantly.

"Typical! Can I expect either of my off-spring to be punctual?" griped Mother Goose.

"Fine. We'll begin without him. Reginald, let's get started."

"Yes, Your Majesty," said Reginald haughtily.

"But Mother, I need to talk to you about something. It's serious."

"No buts, Jillian," said Mother Goose, cutting her daughter off.

Reginald grabbed Jill's right hand with his left hand. He put Jill's left hand on his right shoulder. Finally, he put his right arm around Jill's waist and looked up at her. "The tardy princess will begin with the waltz," he announced. "Ready now…and one, two, three, one, two, three…"

Jill had a wonderful view of the top of Reginald's balding head. This unpleasant experience was made worse by the fact that Reginald wasn't a very good dancer. Jill was trying to get her mother's attention, but it was difficult because Reginald kept stepping on her toes.

"Mother, someone brought me—Ow!—a note this morning."

"The obstinate princess must concentrate," chided Reginald. "One, two, three, one, two, three…"

Jill ignored him. "It came from the land—Ow!—the land of Grimm."

"The unruly princess is not following properly. Feel the rhythm. One, two, three, one, two, three…"

Jill glowered at Reginald. "It appears that—Ow!—it appears that there is a—Ow!—a problem. They want me to—Ow! That's it!" Jill pulled away from the butler. "Mother, if I continue to dance with Reginald, I may end up crippled for life."

Mother Goose would hear none of it. "You seem quite willing to suffer scrapes and bruises as a Royal Guard-in-training."

Jill hated it when her mother made her feel guilty. "Fine!" she shouted angrily, "I'll dance. But this time, Reginald, *I'll* lead!"

Grabbing the butler's hand with a swift jerk, and putting her other arm around his pudgy waist, Jill guided him around the room in graceful rhythmic circles. Reginald was much too embarrassed to protest, which finally allowed Jill to talk to her mother.

As she danced around the great hall, Jill told Mother Goose about the strange situation in the land of Grimm. Mother Goose listened silently. When Jill explained the part about Prince Charming, Mother Goose began to feel anxious. But when Jill reached the part about going to Grimm to help, even though she could be in great danger, Mother Goose shouted, "No, I absolutely forbid it!"

Jill and Reginald stopped dancing.

"Reginald, would you please excuse us," said Mother Goose in her normal voice. "I wish to speak to the princess alone."

Reginald bowed his head before he walked over to the great hall doors. Only Jill saw him stick out his tongue at her as he passed.

When the doors clicked shut behind him, Jill expected her mother to begin another tirade. But Mother Goose said nothing at first. She had learned long ago that she would likely have more success keeping the sun from setting than keeping her spirited daughter from an adventure. It wasn't really a matter of forbidding Jill from going to the land of Grimm. It was a matter of understanding what she intended to do and trying to protect her while she did it.

"I wish you could bring Sir Dumpty along for assistance. It would be much safer. Unfortunately, Sir Dumpty is currently visiting the Great Wall of China. How about taking your brother?" Mother Goose asked.

"The note says that men can't sense that anything is wrong. But I will let Jack know where I am going."

"When Sir Dumpty came to me last year and suggested you might be an excellent addition to the Royal Guard, I had my doubts. I knew you were brave and spirited and as talented as anyone in this kingdom. But I also thought you were reckless and self-absorbed."

"You were right, Mother," said Jill honestly. "I am all those things."

"Your father was very heroic too," Mother Goose continued, "but given a choice, he much preferred gardening to fighting."

Jill had never met her father. Like Jack, she learned about him in bits and pieces from the stories her mother and Sir Dumpty told her. Jill wondered what he would have thought about her, if he were still alive.

Mother Goose finally spoke. "In some ways I am very traditional. A princess should uphold her title with dignity and grace. Your father was of a different opinion. He would have appreciated your unbridled spirit. And perhaps he was right. Let's face it, this is a very strange kingdom. Roving packs of blind mice attack the wives of farmers. Black sheep cut wool off their own backs and divide it into bags. Your mother laughs like a duck and walks like a goose! One princess who doesn't care to wear a dress doesn't exactly stand out."

Jill might not have known what her father thought about her, but she was pretty sure she knew what her mother thought. She ran over and gave Mother Goose a big hug.

"Thank you, Mother," Jill whispered in her ear.

"Be careful, Jillian," Mother Goose whispered back.

As Jill headed toward the door her mother suddenly called out, "You are going into the land of Grimm. It's not the same as our kingdom. Sometimes a sense of humor is the best weapon a person can carry."

Princess Jill steered her horse out of the royal stables and headed north toward the land of Grimm. She had left a letter on Jack's pillow explaining where she was going, but not exactly why. No need to worry him, she figured.

Jill rode through the kingdom, past farmers and craftspeople and minor royalty, past strange folk who leapt over candlesticks and girls who spent their days eating curds on spider-infested furniture. Why did they do it? No one was exactly sure. But Jill didn't mind. Strange is interesting, and interesting is certainly much better than boring.

Before long she was close to the border between the kingdom of Mother Goose and the land of Grimm. There was only one small cottage nearby. Why would anyone want to live so far away and all alone? Jill wondered.

Jill noticed the peculiar garden beside the cottage. It wasn't your typical garden in that it didn't contain anything that actually grew. For instance, one row was made up entirely of cockleshells, and there was a row of tiny silver bells tinkling softly in the breeze. But the oddest of sights was the row of small statues of little girls dressed in maid outfits. There were at least fifty of them, all exactly the same, with white bonnets and aprons over long white dresses. Each maid smiled gaily up at the sky.

Jill's eyes followed the row of cheerful little maids right to the end, where her eyes fell upon the last maid, who was neither small, nor cheerful, nor a statue. She was a real living person wearing a *black* bonnet and apron over a long *black* dress.

The girl had dark hair that fell over her face like a curtain. Her shoulders were bunched up high as if they were trying to keep her earlobes from drooping. There was something brittle about her, Jill thought. The girl, who was about the same age as Jill, was frowning as if there had been a rain cloud over her head since the day she was born.

But Jill needed to get some directions. "I like your garden," she said, attempting to make conversation. "It's very... interesting."

"No, it's not," said the girl, glaring hard.

"Yes, it *is*," insisted Princess Jill stubbornly, glaring right back.

"No, it's *not*," repeated the girl, baring her teeth.

"Yes, it is!" yelled Princess Jill.

"No, it's not!" yelled the girl even louder.

Jill was completely astounded. This girl was the most belligerent, quarrelsome, CONTRARY person in the kingdom...other than herself, that is.

"I said it is!" growled Jill, jumping off her horse.

"And I said it isn't!" returned the girl, rolling up her sleeves and making two fists.

Jill and the girl stood nose to nose, eyeball to eyeball, daring each other to make the first move. Then Jill realized that she couldn't even remember what they were fighting about. For the first time in her life, Princess Jill decided to take the high road and back down from this argument.

"I'm sorry if I offended you. What I really wanted to say is that I am on my way to the land of Grimm, and—"

"No, you're not," interrupted the girl.

"Excuse me? Yes, I certainly am on my way there right now!" said Jill, feeling infuriated.

"No, you're certainly not," replied the girl, jutting out her chin.

For the second time in her life, Jill decided to take the high road. Obviously this girl was just being stubborn and trying to provoke her. Jill would not take the bait. She would not stoop so low. Jill took a deep breath and tried again.

"We seem to be getting off on the wrong foot," said Princess Jill diplomatically.

"Well, I think it's the right foot," replied the girl, making a rude face.

For the third and final time, Jill clawed her way up to the higher road and was determined to stay there. Even though every muscle in Jill's body was screaming for her to jump on the girl's back and force her to say "wrong foot," Jill was going to be better than that. But really, this was the most contrary person she had ever met. No matter what Jill said, this girl would say the opposite. Aha, thought Jill, getting an idea.

"You must be Princess Jill," said Jill to the girl.

"No, I must be Mary," insisted Mary.

Jill smiled. "And I am certainly *not* going to the land of Grimm," she continued.

"You most certainly *are* going to the land of Grimm if you continue toward those trees in the distance," Mary said, as if she had just won a battle.

Now we're getting somewhere, thought Jill. But before she could get back on her horse, she started to feel dizzy again, just like before. There again was the beautiful white horse galloping toward her, and on it was the handsome young man. Again Jill saw the horse and rider jumping over tall hedges, which was strange because a minute before there had been no hedges in sight.

Jill desperately wanted the young man to pick her up in his arms, and she believed she would simply die of sadness if he didn't. She tried to break the image's hold on her brain, but she was powerless. "My prince, I await you!" she called out.

Then suddenly another image flashed before her eyes. It was a castle with glittering lights all over it. There was a large sign hanging above the castle door, but Jill could not read it. She could feel her heart being tugged toward the castle as if she were a puppet. She would have lost control completely except that...

"Ow!" Jill cried out. Mary had pushed her down into the dirt.

"It's rude to just stop arguing with someone!" growled Mary as she stared down at Jill.

Jill wasn't about to fight back. She was grateful for the push. It had broken the spell that might have turned her into a blabbering zombie.

But what about Mary? Why wasn't she controlled by the spell? Jill wondered. Maybe she was so disagreeable that she could resist its power. Jill decided it might be a good idea to keep Mary around to help her snap out of any more trances. It was just too bad that Jill couldn't stand being around her. The high road was certainly an annoying road. Jill sighed.

"Listen up, Mary, because I will only say this once," yelled Jill. "I completely forbid you to get a horse from your stable and ride with me into the land of Grimm. Under no circumstances are you to ever snap me out of another trance. And finally, don't you ever, EVER say that I am smarter, tougher and better than you in every possible way."

Then Jill waited for Mary to ignore her commands and go get her horse.

Jill and Mary crossed over into the land of Grimm. For Jill, it felt like jumping into freezing water. The dark forest began immediately at the border. The tree branches looked like spindly old fingers, all crooked and bony. There was a spooky fog that slithered along the ground like a giant sickly snake. Howls and shrieks cried out from everywhere.

This forest might as well have a sign warning *Danger! Keep Out!* thought Jill.

Farther and farther they rode. The cheerless day faded into a dreary dusk. Hungry and tired, Jill began to wonder if this adventure was such a good idea after all.

You can imagine, then, how strange and wonderful a sight it was to come across a pretty cottage in the middle of all this gloom. Jill was certainly surprised, especially when she discovered that the house was made entirely out of candies, chocolate and cookies.

Jill and Mary jumped off their horses to investigate. They walked along a sugar cube path and up an orange wafer staircase. They came up to a milk chocolate door, and Jill was about to press a marshmallow doorbell, except Mary ate it before she had a chance. Apparently Jill was not the only one who was hungry. Jill would have used the marzipan door knocker except Mary quickly stuffed that in her mouth too.

"Mary, how about you *not* go and eat the toolshed or something?" suggested Jill, not too kindly.

Mary stormed off toward the back of the cottage, but when Jill was just about to rap on the door, she heard a voice coming from behind her.

"Hey you! Skinny kid! Get over here!"

The voice came from inside a cage half-hidden under branches and leaves. Unlike the house, this cage was definitely not made of candy. The bars were solid iron, and a strong padlock kept the door securely shut.

"Who is in there?" asked Jill.

"My name is Hansel," replied the voice.

"What are you doing in there?"

"Oh, you know, the usual story. A witch caught me, locked me up and intends to eat me."

Jill was horrified. "Where I come from, we're not in the habit of eating children."

"Really?" asked Hansel, genuinely surprised. "How odd. Anyway, have you seen my sister or the witch?"

"I heard them," mumbled Mary, who had returned, munching on a drainpipe. "They're in the back of the house."

"I haven't had a crumb to eat all day," Hansel whined. "It's like they've forgotten all about me."

"How about I get the key that opens that lock?" offered Jill.

Then she walked around to the back of the cottage. Never having met a witch before, Jill wasn't sure what to expect. But if eating children was anything to go by...

In the growing darkness, Jill crept along the cottage wall, staying beneath the high windows and out of sight. One open window was lit, and when Jill stood just below it, she heard a raspy voice that reminded her of a shovel dragging along gravel.

"I know what you need, my dear," said the horrible scraping voice. "I know exactly what will spice you up. Trust me, it won't hurt a bit. Ha-ha-ha."

Spice you up? thought Jill in alarm. Oh my! Is the witch planning to eat Gretel instead of her brother?

Jill grabbed the windowsill and pulled herself up high enough to see what was going on.

She still wasn't able to look directly

into the room, but she was able to see the shadows of two figures projected on the far wall. Someone she assumed to be Gretel was sitting down on a chair, tied up. Someone she assumed to be the witch was standing behind Gretel and advancing toward her. Jill could also see something in the witch's hand. It was long. It had sharp teeth. The shadow of the witch was raising the shadow of that object over the shadow of Gretel's head. The witch had a knife! She was going to kill Gretel!

"Stop!" yelled Jill, somersaulting through the window and lunging at the witch before she could stab poor Gretel. With only an inch to spare, Jill, most brave and heroic, managed to wrench the knife out of the witch's bony hand.

However, it wasn't a knife. It was a comb.

"Huh?" said Jill, for Gretel was not tied to the chair at all. She was sitting at a table covered with makeup and hair products and fashion magazines. There were dresses and gowns and all sorts of clothes draped over every piece of furniture.

Jill also saw that the witch was wearing a bright pink polka-dot dress with a pointy polka-dot hat. She had a long pink feather boa wrapped around her neck. Add to that the bright pink lipstick, and Jill didn't think the witch looked so much scary or dangerous as she looked, well, ridiculous.

What Jill did *not* see were any spices or herbs or carving knives or cooking pots big enough to put a small girl into. She didn't see anything to suggest that she had just saved Gretel from becoming a witch's dinner. Jill didn't feel so much brave and heroic anymore as she felt, well, ridiculous.

"If you needed a comb, you might have just asked," said the witch sweetly.

"But aren't you going to cook up this girl and eat her?" asked Jill.

"Certainly not!" replied the witch. "Where do people get these ideas?"

"And Hansel," continued Jill, just to make sure. "You're not going to eat Hansel either?"

"Oooh, I completely forgot about him," said the witch. "Well, yes, Hansel I was going to eat, but now I just don't have the time. Do you want to cook him?"

Jill shook her head vigorously.

"In that case, would you be a dear and let him out for me?" said the witch, handing Jill the key that hung around her neck. "Gretel and I are much too busy."

But just after the witch handed over the key, she and Gretel began chanting. "My prince! My prince! Come and take me away!"

"Uh-oh," thought Jill. "Here we go again."

Thinking fast, Jill stuck her head out the window and yelled, "Mary! Whatever you do, do not come into this room and help me!"

Jill braced herself for another trance like someone who had just been warned of an approaching tidal wave. She grabbed onto a dresser with both hands and shut her eyes. It wasn't long before Jill saw the white stallion and handsome prince galloping toward her. Then the image changed and Jill saw the castle with all the lights around it. She could see the sign over the door, and this time she could read part of it. It said: When Only the Best Will Do.

Jill fought the spell with all her strength. It helped for her to remember that she was standing inside the witch's cottage and that it was impossible for the horse to be galloping toward her in a field. It isn't really happening, she told herself. It's not real. But it didn't matter. The spell was becoming too strong to resist.

"My prince! My prince!" Jill called out with open arms. "Come and take me—Ow!"

Mary hit Jill over the head with the cottage mailbox. Just like the cage that held Hansel, this wasn't made of candy either.

"Ow," moaned Jill again, rubbing her head. "You know, Mary, how about next time you just shake me."

"Oh look, Gretel, our invitations to the royal ball have finally arrived!" The witch bent down and picked up an envelope that had fallen out of the mailbox, which was now dented in the shape of Jill's head. She ripped it open and pulled out two invitations.

"Boo-hoo-hoo!" cried Gretel. "We won't be ready in time. We don't have the right clothes. Our hairstyles are wrong. We don't even have perfume."

"You're right, Gretel, we'll look horrible! Prince Charming will be choosing his princess. You can't just wear any old rag to such an occasion, when only the best will do." The witch began to sob uncontrollably too.

Jill flinched. "When only the best will do," she repeated under her breath. "Why does that sound familiar?"

It was getting late. Jill decided that it would be best to spend the night at the cottage. She left Gretel and the witch to continue crying. It was giving her a headache. She went outside and let Hansel out of the cage. Then she went into the kitchen and prepared something to eat that wasn't candy and that didn't contain any bits of children. Remembering to tell Mary not to eat anything, Jill sat down at the kitchen table with Mary and Hansel and they all had some dinner.

Afterward Jill found a chair by the fireplace to curl up in. She wondered about the trances and what was causing them. She wondered who F.G. was and when they would finally meet. In a matter of minutes, tired Princess Jill fell fast asleep.

The next morning, Jill couldn't wait to get out of that cottage. Gretel and the witch were still chattering on about the royal ball, and Hansel was demanding to be fed breakfast. Enough was enough.

Jill gave Hansel a bowl and a spoon and pushed him toward the kitchen. She rounded up Mary and without saying any goodbyes, the two girls mounted their horses and rode away from the candy cottage.

Jill decided that since F.G. hadn't yet found her, she would simply have to find F.G. But then something caught her attention.

"Hey look," said Jill, "there's a lighthouse way over there."

In the distance stood a tall, thin, round tower that indeed looked very much like a lighthouse. It had a window at the very top where a strong lamp might shine through.

"That's not a lighthouse," Mary sneered.

Or perhaps it wasn't a lighthouse. After all, lighthouses are usually built near large bodies of water to warn ships to stay clear of dangerous rocks. This tower was nowhere near any water. It was a strange tower too, because it did not seem to have a door. And there was no lamp in the window. There was only a girl with long blond hair.

"See?" said Mary, who, although contrary, was actually right.

As Jill and Mary guided their horses into a clump of trees in order to observe from a safe place, a young man popped out from behind a bush. After checking to make sure that the coast was clear, he approached the tower and called up to the top, "Rapunzel, Rapunzel, let down thy hair."

Perhaps you have heard the expression "too much of a good thing." It means that something delightful, when taken in great quantities, can have the opposite effect. For example, eating a piece of candy can be a good thing. But eating an entire house made out of candy can make one extremely ill, which is not a good thing.

The girl at the top of the tower had beautiful blond hair. However, as she allowed her hair to flow down the side of the tower, it did not stop. It just kept coming out the window. Her flaxen tresses fell lower and lower until the ends actually reached to where the young man stood waiting. So, to repeat: nice shiny shoulder-length hair is a good thing, but nice shiny hair long enough to hang your laundry on is "too much of a good thing."

The young man grabbed onto the girl's hair, and then fist over fist, he pulled himself up the tower's stone wall. But when the young man had reached the halfway point, the long-haired girl was joined by an older woman who leaned over and whispered something in her ear. This caused the girl to start crying buckets of tears. Then the woman took out an extremely long pair of scissors and placed the blades near the girl's neck. With several sharp snips, she cut the long golden hair to about shoulder length.

Although the girl looked so much better with shorter hair, this was probably not the best time to cut it. The young man fell to the ground with a resounding *whomp*!

"My leg!" he moaned.

Jill sped to his assistance and checked the young man's leg just the way she had learned in her Royal Guard first-aid course. "Your ankle is sprained," Jill explained. "You won't be able to walk on it for a while."

"But Rapunzel is still up in the tower with that horrible witch!" the young man cried frantically. "I must rescue Rapunzel before it's too late."

"I'll take care of it," said Jill, "but first, tell me, are you Prince Charming?"

"Me? Oh, no. I'm Prince Herbert. Prince Charming lives in the huge castle near the town. At least I think he still lives there. No one has seen him for quite some time. Now, please help my love if you can. That witch is horrible. She's kept Rapunzel locked in that tower for years."

What is it with these witches? wondered Jill. After spitting on both her hands for traction, Jill began to climb the tower wall, stone by stone. Her fingers clung onto any jutting bit of rock she could use. Her feet wedged into any small crevice. As she came closer to the window, she could hear the witch threatening Rapunzel.

"Stop moving about, my dear. I'll cut two feet off you and then you can blubber all you want."

Cut her two feet off? thought Jill in a panic. Oh my! Chopping Rapunzel's hair was just the beginning. The horrible witch intends to shorten Rapunzel at both ends!

Jill grabbed the awning just above the window and swung herself into the room.

With only an inch to spare, Jill, most brave and heroic, managed to wrench the long scissors out of the witch's bony hand.

However, it wasn't Rapunzel's feet that the witch was cutting off. It was the hem of Rapunzel's dress.

"Huh?" said Jill, somewhat embarrassed.

"If you thought her gown should remain long, you just had to say so," said the witch.

"You weren't by any chance intending to cut off Rapunzel's feet after you fixed her dress?" asked Jill meekly.

"Certainly not!" exclaimed the witch. "Where do people get these ideas?"

"And the tower? You haven't kept Rapunzel locked in this tower for years?"

"Oh, well, that I did. But I had to. Her mother ate some of my precious plants, and I took her firstborn as payment. It seemed fair at the time."

"I see," said Jill, not really meaning it.

"Fix my dress, witch!" demanded Rapunzel. "My dress must match my hair."

"Yes, the hair!" said Jill, suddenly remembering. "I saw the witch whisper something to you before she snipped most of it off."

"All I said was that Prince Charming prefers short hair," said the witch defensively.

"Boo-hoo-hoo!" cried Rapunzel again. "I thought I would absolutely die when I heard the news. It was the worst moment of my entire life."

"Not nearly as awful as it was for Prince Herbert," said Jill without sympathy.

"Prince Herbert?" asked Rapunzel, wrinkling up her nose.

Jill was confused. "You don't like Prince Herbert?

"Oh, he's all right. I know he would do anything for me and that we have a great time together and we're the closest of friends. But still, he's certainly no Prince Charming."

"What a horrible place this land of Grimm is," Jill sighed, staring out the window.

"I heard that all the women in Grimm have been invited to the ball," the witch prattled on. "I guess that includes Cinderella."

"Ach! Don't mention Cinderella!" screamed Rapunzel. "She has a fairy god-mother to help her get Prince Charming. She's a cheater!"

"Fairy godmother," repeated Jill to herself. "Fairy. Godmother. F. G. Of course! She must be the one who sent me the note."

"My prince! My prince! Come and take me away!" Jill heard voices coming from behind her.

She turned away from the window and saw Rapunzel and the witch with their arms straight out before them. Uh-oh, another spell, she thought.

As before, just at the moment when the prince was close enough to touch Jill, there was a sudden switch to the image

49

he castle with the flashing lights. This
le Jill could read more of the sign above
e door. It said:

shElves of Splendor, Aisles of Bliss
We Have the spRite Stuff
When Only the Best Will Do

There was a tiny part of Jill's brain that
wanted to know if Mary, who was down
at the bottom of the tower, was going to
be able to save her before the powerful
spell overwhelmed her.

"My prince!" Jill called out along with
Rapunzel, the witch and most likely all
the other women in Grimm. "My prince!
Come and—Ouch!"

A ball of dirt flew in the tower's
window and hit Jill square on the
head. Apparently Mary had quite the
arm. And it worked. It broke the spell.
Nonetheless, Jill intended to have a few
words with Mary later. Surely there was
a less painful way to go about this.

Jill shook Rapunzel and the witch.
"How do I find Cinderella?"

"It's simple," replied the witch, as if nothing had happened. "You travel west until you get into town, and then you turn right at the cobbler's shop. Then you—"

"Stop talking! I need help!" whined Rapunzel. "Oh, what's the use anyway? I need a store with shelves full of splendid things!"

Jill was sick of Rapunzel's bellyaching, and, sadly, Jill didn't always take the high road. As she climbed through the window and carefully began lowering herself down the side of the tower, she stopped to say, "By the way, Rapunzel, I heard on great authority that Prince Charming absolutely adores long hair and will marry the girl with the longest hair. Too bad you just cut yours."

Jill could hear Rapunzel's hysterical sobbing all the way down to the ground.

Jill and Mary got on their horses and followed the witch's directions into the town. It was a charming place, but eerily quiet. They trotted along the main road and saw very few people. Both sides were lined with tidy stores and respectable businesses, but nothing was really open. Many shopkeepers sat on their stoops, looking bored or depressed. At one corner, Jill recognized the cobbler's shop by the big boot-shaped sign swinging above the front window. The cobbler was sitting on his doorstep, smoking a pipe.

Jill nodded to the man. "Good day to you, sir."

"Oh? What's so good about it?" the man replied sullenly. "I haven't sold a pair of shoes in weeks."

"I'm sorry to hear that," said Jill. "Business is slow for you lately?"

"Not just for me. For all the stores in town. Everyone is saying our wares aren't good enough anymore. They say that only the best will do."

There's that phrase again, thought Jill.

"Serves us right," continued the man. "We all got lazy about our chores."

"How come?" asked Jill, who knew all about being lazy when it came to chores.

The man stood up and sauntered over to them. "I suppose I shouldn't be telling you this, but since I'll likely be selling my shop, it probably doesn't matter."

Jill and Mary leaned forward. "Tell us what?"

"I stopped making shoes a long time ago. I don't mean that I didn't sell shoes. Oh, I sold a lot of shoes and made a pretty penny for them. But I didn't make them. I had help. Secret help."

The two girls were really intrigued now. They leaned over even farther. "Secret help?" they both asked.

"Elves," said the cobbler. "Elves were making my shoes. All I did was get the material, and then they would make them for me at night. They work fast, the wee folk, and don't take breaks. The best part was that I didn't even have to pay them. I just threw them a few crumbs and they were fine. Same with all the other shops in town. Elves! They did the work and we got the money."

"The elves weren't upset?" asked Jill.

"We didn't think so at the time. But they must have been bothered because they've disappeared. Haven't seen one little elf in weeks. And now we're all ruined."

"No you're not," disagreed Mary. "Just go back to making your own shoes."

Even Jill couldn't argue with that. But the cobbler shook his head. "Can't. I don't remember how."

Suddenly there was a loud commotion as a group of five hunters ran down the street toward them. Each one had a bow in his hand and a quiver of arrows on his back. The first hunter to arrive looked desperately toward the cobbler.

"Any sign of our lost companion?" he asked.

The cobbler shook his head. "I haven't seen a soul all day except for these young ladies," he replied, indicating Jill and Mary.

"Then that makes four hunters missing," said the second hunter as the rest of the group gathered around. "Five, if you include Prince Charming."

"Can't say for sure about the prince," countered the first. "He's been missing a lot longer. But it's true. They all disappeared on his property."

"All gone," said the third hunter. "You know what this reminds me of?"

At this, the hunters grew quiet. Finally the eldest, who had grizzled hair and a weathered face, spoke up. "Aye. It be Iron Hans, no question. The monster has returned to our poor land once more."

"Dear sirs, excuse my nosiness," said Jill, "but I am a stranger to Grimm. Please tell me—who is this Iron Hans person?"

"Person?" said the eldest hunter, turning toward Jill. "Iron Hans is no person, missy. Iron Hans is a huge wild animal on two legs. A beast without a soul. Long ago, many fine hunters were lost to this creature, never to return to their families. He has unimaginable strength."

"And wealth," added the first hunter.

"And magic," added the second.

"Aye," agreed the eldest hunter. "Powerful magic."

"But we were told that it was all a curse; that he was freed from it and returned to being just a man," said the third hunter. "We thought this was all done with long ago."

"Why is he called Iron Hans?" asked Jill.

"Because under the long dirty hair that covers his body is rancid skin the color of rusted metal."

"Oh," said Jill, really wishing she hadn't asked.

The hunters bowed politely to Jill, Mary and the cobbler, then continued on their way, with bows and arrows at the ready. Jill and Mary, after getting directions to Cinderella's house, bid farewell to the cobbler.

"I don't know how people can live here," complained Jill. "First, it looks as if Prince Charming is using magic to control the minds of all the women and girls. Then there are all these witches doing horribly nasty things. Now there is this scary Iron Hans beast making hunters disappear."

"And there are elves too," added Mary.

"That's true," agreed Jill. "The hunters didn't know about the elves."

"Help us! Stop, please! Help us!" Jill heard a chorus of voices.

Up ahead, the path was blocked by seven very upset little men. As the girls approached, they swarmed around the horses.

Jill sighed. "What is it now?"

"Our dear Snow White, the most beautiful woman in all of Grimm, is being held hostage in our cottage," the seven dwarves explained, quite remarkably, all at the same time.

"By whom?" asked Jill.

"By the vainest and most evil woman in all the land," answered six of the dwarves.

"Not to mention the most insecure," added the seventh.

"But why don't you just make her go away?" asked Jill. "It is, after all, your house."

"We can't! She's bolted the door and barricaded it with furniture. She's sealed and covered the windows. She's even started a fire in the hearth so no one can climb down the chimney."

Six of the dwarves began to sob inconsolably.

"If only we hadn't left our pickaxes in the cottage. Then we could have broken down the door," lamented the seventh dwarf. Then he started sobbing too. But the other six dwarves suddenly stopped.

"Of course!" the six yelled happily. "We

could use the mine shaft that runs right under the cottage."

"Why do you have a mine shaft under your house?" asked Mary.

"We were new to mining at the time," the six dwarves explained bashfully. "The shaft was supposed to go into the mountain where the diamonds were, but we got a bit dopey with the directions."

"You know, I don't think we'll still fit in the mine shaft," said the seventh dwarf, rubbing his round tummy.

"He's right," agreed the other six well-fed dwarves. "We need someone scrawny to fit in the mine shaft. Someone like..."

Seven sets of hopeful eyes turned toward Jill.

"Fine! Lead the way," grumbled scrawny Princess Jill.

The two girls followed the seven dwarves down a winding path through the forest to the entrance of a diamond mine set into the foot of a steep mountain. The entrance was framed with timber boards and beams, and it was tall enough for

Jill to walk through while standing up straight. This encouraged her a great deal, because she had imagined the mine shaft being so low that she might have to crawl through it on her hands and knees.

"So I just continue along this shaft and it will take me under your cottage, right?" Jill asked.

"Oh, no," chorused the seven dwarves as they pushed aside a modest-sized boulder to reveal another mine shaft, which was much smaller and far narrower. "You need to use this one."

"That's absolutely wonderful," said Jill, not even close to meaning it.

Jill inched her way down the much smaller mine shaft on her hands and knees. Sometimes she paused to clear her throat of all the dust she had swallowed. Sometimes she paused to pick off slimy bugs that had fallen into her hair. But mainly Jill paused to yell the kind of things that princesses should never say in the company of others.

Eventually the mine shaft came to an abrupt halt. The cottage must be right above, Jill figured. She pulled away a few loose rocks from above her head. Then she wiped away the large pile of dirt that fell on her face. Then she yelled something that made even the earth-worms blush.

With the rocks and dirt cleared away, Jill carefully made a hole just under the kitchen table. She poked her head up through the hole.

"What is going on?" she whispered to herself.

The sight before her was most bizarre. A tall imposing lady stood at the far end of the cottage. She wore a black velvet dress that matched her black hair and her even blacker mood. She had a scary face. A really scary face. To be fair, it might have looked less scary if it hadn't looked so insanely angry.

The scary lady was holding an eyebrow tweezer in one hand and a mirror in her other. And she was yelling at it. That's right—she was yelling at the mirror.

"How about now?!" she shouted.

"No, she's still much more beautiful," the mirror replied simply (and quite remarkably).

"Agggghhhh!" screamed the woman.

Then she took the eyebrow tweezer and pulled out several eyebrow hairs, one by painful one. "How about now?!"

"Definitely an improvement, but I would still have to say that Snow White is more beautiful." If the scary lady hadn't been so wound up and excited, she might have noted a touch of mischief in the mirror's voice. "Might I suggest you work on some of those nose hairs?" said the mirror.

With her eyes still just above the floor, Jill finally spotted Snow White slumped in one of the kitchen chairs.

If she was as beautiful as the dwarves and the mirror said, it was certainly hard to tell, because Snow White's head was tilted backward, her mouth was wide open, and a little drool was dribbling out the side, which is never attractive. Jill noticed that the young woman's arms hung lifeless at her sides and a half-eaten apple lay on the floor beside her. On the kitchen counter directly behind Snow White was a small blue bottle with a skull and crossbones on the label.

Poison, thought Jill. The scary lady has poisoned Snow White. She needs medical help before it's too late, if it isn't too late already.

Jill chose to be brave and heroic one more time. She hoisted herself up out of the mine shaft and then she lunged at the scary lady, wrenching the mirror out of her hand.

"Give it back!" barked the scary lady.

"Not until you tell me how to reverse the effects of the poison."

"But I didn't poison her!" the scary lady exclaimed indignantly.

At that instant, Jill heard a very loud yawn. She turned around to see Snow White sit up, eyes wide open and presumably alive. "I thought you were dead," said Jill frantically.

"Well, I was nearly bored to death," said Snow White, standing and stretching. "She's been at this for hours. I guess I fell asleep sometime after the mirror suggested she scrub her tongue with laundry soap."

"And I'm still not more beautiful than you," cried the scary lady. "How will Prince Charming ever notice me at the ball if I'm not the most beautiful?"

"The dwarves thought you were going to kill Snow White," explained Jill.

"Those pesky dwarves! I need Snow White *alive* in order for me to know if I'm more beautiful!" shouted the scary lady.

"I'm sorry," said Jill, handing back the mirror. "I saw the bottle of poison on the counter and I just assumed the worst."

"It's true, I had intended on poisoning her *earlier*. I thought of all kinds of ways to kill Snow White," the scary lady continued. "Dreadful ways. But then I realized it wasn't in my best interests."

This was the final straw for Jill. Having put herself through pain and misery for the third time, Jill lost all patience. She was a lit piece of dynamite with no more fuse. "You *were* going to poison her? Or worse?" she yelled at the scary lady. "I've said it once, I'll say it a thousand times: What is wrong with you witches?"

"But she isn't a witch," said Snow White. "She's my stepmother."

"Agggghhhh!" screamed Jill.

Jill was livid. She was trembling with anger.

"That's it! I've had it with this place!" Jill screamed as she stomped over to the door. One by one, Jill tossed aside the seven small beds stacked against it. She unbolted the door, kicked it open and marched outside.

"This place is nuts!" Jill ranted. "The people here are nuts!"

Jill stormed right past the seven dwarves and Mary without even looking at them. She carried on straight into the woods.

"What did I get myself into? Why should I help them? Half of them are trying to find horrible things to do to the other half! So what's the point? There is no point! Stepmothers killing their stepdaughters? Witches eating children? These people are beyond help! Well, I'm out of here!"

However, it was impossible for Jill to be out of there, because she was now lost.

She had been so caught up in her temper tantrum that she had paid no attention to where she was going. She had no clue as to where she was other than that she was among a lot of trees and ferns.

"Oh, this is really, really great," said Jill, not really, really meaning it.

Like Jill, you are probably thinking it can't get any worse than this. I am almost reluctant to mention that at this low moment, another spell started to seep into Jill's mind. But without Mary by her side, Jill had no one to snap her out of it.

There in front of her was the prince, riding his familiar white stallion closer and closer. Tired, upset and confused, Jill knew she had no strength to fight it this time. She could feel her will slipping away, and she knew she was doomed to become another zombie like Gretel and Rapunzel and all the others.

The stallion galloped closer and closer. The prince looked so amazing, so handsome. Jill stood defeated, waiting for him to scoop her up and carry her to the beautiful castle with all the lights and the strange sign. He was very close now. He was leaning forward on his horse and his hand was reaching toward her. Jill could feel a hand on her shoulder. Gently, it held her and shook. Back and forth the hand shook her until Jill slowly opened her eyes and awoke from the trance.

"Hello, Jill," said a kind-looking woman in a shimmering dress. "I'm F.G."

"Fairy Godmother," Jill whispered before she fainted dead away.

Upon waking up for the second time, Jill found herself on the ground, but with her head resting in Fairy Godmother's lap.

"Feeling better now?" she asked Jill.

"I guess so," replied Jill, sitting up slowly. "My throat is a bit dry."

"No doubt from all that yelling you did. I don't have a lot of magic these days, but I think I can whip something up for you." And with that, Fairy Godmother made a tall glass of lemonade appear out of thin air. Or, to be honest, she conjured up a glass with several unpeeled lemons squished into it.

"That's not what I wanted to do. Hold on," said Fairy Godmother. With a nod, she made the glass of lemons disappear and instead turned Jill into a lemon tree.

"No, no, no," she sighed. But rather than turning Jill back into herself, she turned her into a big lemon with arms and legs sticking out.

"I can fix that," said Fairy Godmother, looking slightly embarrassed. She finally changed Jill back to normal. "Sorry. Something is interfering with my magic. Shall I try again?"

"No, no, that's okay," insisted Jill, who was afraid she might end up as a lemon meringue pie. "But thank you, anyway."

"Thank you for coming to rescue us, Jill," said Fairy Godmother. "I believe I chose wisely in asking for your help. But you have had a rough couple of days."

"I don't want to be disrespectful, but this place is horrible. There is so much mean stuff going on all the time."

Fairy Godmother smiled warmly at Jill. "I see. Grimm doesn't make a lot of sense to you, does it? But someone coming into your mother's kingdom might find all of you different too. Is that Pumpkin Eater fellow still treating his wife poorly?"

"Oh, no. He and his wife worked it out. He's Peter Salad Eater now," replied Jill.

"And Georgie-Porgie? Is he still kissing any girl he chooses?"

"Oh, I'm pretty sure I took care of that nasty habit."

"Perhaps, Jill, with a little time and support, Grimm can work out its problems too."

Fairy Godmother stood up, and for the first time Jill had a chance to really look at her. Fairy Godmother was tall. Her dress was sizable but looked as light as air, and it was as sparkly as Red had described it. There was a glow about Fairy Godmother that brightened everything around her.

"Jill, I would like you to meet someone who might offer you a little hope in the land of Grimm. Then you can decide whether you still wish to help us or not." Then she turned around and tiptoed through the forest. From behind, Jill could see the small delicate wings on Fairy Godmother's back.

While they walked, Jill told Fairy Godmother everything she had learned so far. She told her all about the spells with the image of the castle adorned with lights.

She told her how all the women she met kept trying to make themselves look beautiful but never seemed to be satisfied. And she told her about the shopkeepers and the elves.

"I'm not surprised about the elves doing their work," nodded Fairy Godmother. "Elves are very industrious and very clever too. I have known some elves to make absolutely amazing objects—even machines. But it's unlike them to disappear. Even if they were upset with the shopkeepers, they would have given some warning. They're very proper about such things."

Finally Jill told Fairy Godmother about Iron Hans.

"Now that's surprising," said Fairy Godmother thoughtfully. "Iron Hans back in the land of Grimm? He's powerful, that one. And greedy."

"Perhaps Prince Charming and Iron Hans are conspiring together," offered Jill.

Before long, Jill and Fairy Godmother were at the banks of a river. A young woman, perhaps six or seven years older than Jill, was kneeling at the water's edge washing a dress. There was a large basket of elegant clothes beside her— much nicer than the clothes she was wearing. She was scrubbing very hard, and she looked very tired.

"Jill, I would like to introduce you to Cinderella," said Fairy Godmother.

Cinderella turned her head toward Jill and gave a small smile.

"So you're Jill," said Cinderella. "Fairy Godmother said you might come to help. Although we disagree about what needs fixing."

"Why, the Prince Charming spell, of course," said Jill.

Cinderella sat down on a rock and sighed heavily. Jill turned to Fairy Godmother for an explanation.

"She doesn't seem affected by the spell," said Fairy Godmother. "Cinderella and Prince Charming have known each other for a long time. They are deeply in love. Perhaps true love protects her from the spell's power."

"But everyone says he intends to pick a bride at the ball tomorrow," Jill stated a little reluctantly.

"I know him. He wouldn't do that by choice." Cinderella turned to Jill and looked her straight in the eye. "I haven't seen him in over a week, and I'm very worried. I don't dare ask anyone about him because no one except F.G. knows about our love. As far as most people are concerned, I am just my stepmother's lowly servant."

"We could resolve this right now if I could just take a look inside his castle," lamented Fairy Godmother, "but something is preventing me from using most of my magic. The only thing I can do right is make myself two inches tall, which is fairly useless. I can't even fly, otherwise I'd sneak in through a window."

"And the castle butler has been given strict orders not to allow anyone to enter the castle until the royal ball. That's two nights away," added Cinderella.

Everyone was taking a thoughtful pause when Mary came crashing through the trees pulling both horses behind her.

"There you are!" she shouted. Then she blushed and stared down at her feet, mumbling, "I mean, I'm glad you're okay and all."

Jill was touched by Mary's concern.

"It's getting late," said Fairy Godmother. "I suggest we leave things as they are for today. There is an abandoned cottage not far from here where you and Mary can sleep."

Cinderella picked up her heavy basket of laundry. "I should get back home before my stepmother and stepsisters begin to wonder where I am. It doesn't take much for them to get upset with me. I'll see you tomorrow, Jill, if you still intend to help us."

"I do," said Jill.

"Wonderful!" exclaimed Fairy God-mother. Then she kissed Cinderella on the forehead. "You see? Things are working out. Not to worry."

Cinderella gave everyone a polite smile and headed off to her stepmother's house.

"Tomorrow Mary and I will look around Prince Charming's forest, where the hunters went missing," Jill decided. "But first thing in the morning, I need to get into the castle."

Jill stood at the edge of the deep moat that surrounded Prince Charming's castle. She was about to do something very immature and possibly dangerous.

But Jill was confronted by a strange sight. The castle was covered in scaffolding and draped with longs sheets of dark fabric. She could hear the sound of hammers and saws coming from behind the cloth. However, what was being built was anyone's guess.

There was something else that was strange too. The metal flagpole atop one of the castle turrets was very, very high. In fact, the flagpole was so outrageously high that Jill bet she could see all the way to Mother Goose's kingdom from its top.

"Why would anyone need such a tall flagpole?" Jill puzzled. She pulled on a long rope that stretched across the moat and rang the castle doorbell. Then she ran behind a tree and hid.

The drawbridge came down. At the doorway stood a stiff frowning man, whom Jill assumed to be the royal butler. The butler looked around, shrugged his shoulders and then pulled the drawbridge up again.

Jill ran and pulled on the rope once more and scrambled back to the tree just as the drawbridge reopened. This time the butler walked across the drawbridge to the other side. Jill could see that he was very displeased. The butler put his hands on his hips, searched all around and finally gave up and went back inside. The drawbridge closed behind him.

"Here we go," said Jill, gathering up all her courage.

Once more she rang the bell and hid behind the tree. This time the drawbridge fell open immediately and the butler ran across the drawbridge yelling, "I know someone is there! Think you're so clever, do you?"

As the butler hunted in the surrounding woods, Jill snuck behind him and scrambled, unseen, across the drawbridge and into the castle.

The place appeared completely empty. She passed no one in the halls or on the staircases. She heard not a peep from any of the rooms.

She passed one door that was covered with large signs saying *Keep Out!* and *Do Not Enter Under Any Circumstances!* and *I Mean It!* However, the door was unlocked and slightly ajar, which made all the threatening signs seem, well, silly. Jill pushed gently against the door.

The room was filled with a lot of strange machines. They were big and shiny and made occasional beeping sounds. One machine had a screen showing an image of the prince riding his galloping white horse over hedges. Then it switched to an image of the castle covered with lights. Over and over, the screen shifted from one image to the other.

The large flagpole that Jill had seen outside actually came through a hole in the roof and down into this room. It must be connected to all of this, Jill realized.

But there was another machine, and it would most likely have gone unnoticed were it not for the sign that read *Brain-Hypnotizing Machine*. Upon it were two buttons. One button was labeled *Women of Grimm*. The other button said *Princess Jill*.

"This must be what is causing the spells," Jill thought.

Jill was about to turn off the machine when she heard footsteps in the hallway. She hid behind the machines, afraid that the butler might find her. Sure enough, the footsteps came right into the room, accompanied by two voices. Because Jill was crouched down, she couldn't see who was speaking. All she could see were two pointy hats.

"He's so mean!" said one voice. "If we're not careful, he'll kill us without any remorse."

"At least we're not kept in that dirty dungeon like the rest of those poor souls," said the other voice.

"And what about Prince Charming, imprisoned in a tower in his own castle? We should try to escape now, before it's too late!"

"Bite your tongue. We follow orders unless we want our beloved leader to die a horrible death. By tomorrow night it will all be over and everyone will be safe. Now let's get this machine going. It's time for the mid-morning trance."

"What message are we sending them now?" groaned the first voice.

"Apparently we tell them to bring all their money, their gold and their jewels to the royal ball if they want to marry Prince Charming," answered the second voice. "Poor Prince Charming," he added.

So it's true. Prince Charming is not involved in any of this, thought Jill. Maybe I should try to find him before I leave the castle.

Taking a deep breath, she silently slipped out from behind the machines and through the door without being noticed. Jill climbed up every floor until she found the one final staircase that spiraled up to Prince Charming's room.

Jill tapped lightly on the door. "Prince Charming, are you in there?"

"Go away!" shouted a voice from inside.

"I bring regards from Cinderella," Jill said.

In a flash, the door opened up just wide enough for two eyes to peer out. "Did you say Cinderella?" asked Prince Charming.

"Yes, I did," nodded Jill.

Prince Charming was silent as he poked his head out the door and looked in every direction. When he was sure they were completely alone, he opened the door and beckoned Jill inside. "Hurry!"

Prince Charming was an older boy, perhaps eighteen or so, who looked very worried and upset.

"If anyone discovers me talking to you, my mother and father will be in great danger," explained Prince Charming.

"I didn't see one other person in the whole castle," remarked Jill. "I did hear two voices though, and I saw the tops of a couple of pointy hats.

"They're elves," Prince Charming explained. "Iron Hans has their leader locked in the dungeon along with my parents. He has threatened to kill them all if I don't cooperate. The elves are very loyal to their leader. He forced two of them to make the dungeon escape-proof. No one has seen those elves since. I'm supposed to stay alone in my room until this is all over."

"Until what is all over?" Jill asked.

"Tomorrow night is the royal ball. Iron Hans has spread the rumor that I will choose my princess bride there. All the women in the kingdom are invited, but before they can get into the ballroom, Iron Hans has figured out a way to make the women hand over all their money and gold."

"How will he do that?" asked Jill.

"I'm not quite sure. But after he gets his riches, he promises to free my parents and the elf leader."

"Can Iron Hans be trusted to keep his promise?" Jill wondered.

"I would never trust that monster," spat Prince Charming. "But what choice do I have? He's terribly powerful, and I have no army to fight him."

Jill wished she could say something positive, but it was a dismal situation for Prince Charming.

"Cinderella is very worried about you," she offered. "She always believed you were innocent."

That made Prince Charming smile. "If Cinderella came to the ball tomorrow, I would ask *her* to be my bride. But that's impossible. Her stepmother would never allow it."

"Prince Charming, I promise you that I will do whatever I can to help. Do not lose hope."

And with that, Jill and Prince Charming shook hands.

After Jill left Prince Charming in his room, she met Mary at the back of the castle and together they explored the royal forest.

Like all forests in Grimm, this one was dense and gloomy. It was probably haunted as well, Jill thought, because she could hear many tiny voices carried upon the wind. They sounded like little whispers or sad songs. Frankly, it gave her the willies. But not Mary. She just scowled as usual.

"Mary, don't you ever get even a little bit scared?" Jill asked.

"I've lived alone for a long time. I used to be scared, but not anymore."

"But why *do* you live alone?" asked Jill.

Mary was about to tell Jill to mind her own business, but she could see that Jill was truly interested. So she said something else instead. "I wasn't born contrary, Princess Jill. I wasn't always unfriendly. But I'm a bit different from all the other little maids. That made things difficult for me. So I choose to live alone."

I'm certainly different too, thought Jill, but perhaps no one dares make things difficult for a princess.

Deeper into the woods, almost hidden from view by a tall thicket, they discovered a long wooden cabin covered with a mossy roof. Jill and Mary crawled up to a window and peered inside. They saw rows and rows of tables piled with different fabrics. Along the tables were many elves sitting on tall stools, bent over and working at a frantic pace. They were measuring and cutting, sewing and cobbling and stuffing things into boxes. None of the elves looked happy at all.

At the far end of the room was a mound of what could only be described as tangled black hair and rusted metal parts. Whatever the elves could fashion out of those disgusting materials was anybody's guess.

Jill noticed that the mound was moving. The top slowly lifted up and showed itself to be a head. A large head with a horrible face. A face like an ogre's with glowing green eyes, two bottom teeth that stuck out like fangs, and a nose that looked like it could smell fear a mile away. The green eyes scanned the room menacingly.

"Iron Hans," Jill whispered in awe.

Iron Hans slowly rose up. Jill could now see the beast in its awful entirety. Iron Hans stood seven feet tall, even with his hunched back. His feet were as huge as a giant's, and he walked with long deliberate steps. As he made his way down the aisles between the tables, each little elf cowered and trembled.

"Hurry, you little runts!" he shouted, "Everything must be ready to sell before the royal ball begins."

"But sir, if we rush, the quality of our work will suffer," observed an older bearded elf.

"What do I care about quality?" bellowed Iron Hans. "Stitch them together so they last only one night. After that they can fall to pieces, for all I care."

A hubbub of shocked voices spread around the room. Apparently, for elves, such disregard for quality was like using very bad language in front of your grand-mother.

Then Iron Hans walked over to the door. "And one more thing, my pointy-heads," he growled. "One of you better have a horse and cart parked at the back of the castle tomorrow night. A strong cart! Because it will be carrying a lot of gold. A LOT OF GOLD!" Iron Hans laughed so loudly that the workshop windows shook and a few of the younger elves bounced off their stools and onto the floor.

"Yikes," said Jill softly.

"Double yikes," added Mary, who had just remembered what it felt like to be scared.

They flattened themselves against the cabin wall as Iron Hans stepped outside. He stopped and sniffed the air. For a second, Jill thought they were done for, but Iron Hans just shrugged and stomped off into the woods toward the castle.

When he was a safe distance away, Jill and Mary began to follow him. Iron Hans came to an open space covered in dried leaves. He reached down into the leaves and grabbed a ring-shaped handle. Then, with a grunt, he pulled the handle with one powerful heave and a large metal door swung open with a thundering boom.

"How are my little pets doing?" he sneered into the hole.

An arm reached up out of the darkness. "Please, Iron Hans, let us go," said a very weak-sounding voice. "We promise not to say anything."

"So sorry, my dear hunters, but I cannot risk anyone ruining my plans. Too bad you stumbled across my workshop."

"We'll starve to death," groaned another voice.

"Oh, not to worry, not to worry," said Iron Hans with mock concern. "Look, I brought you food. This should keep you fed for another day, or week, or however long it takes for you to be rescued." He dropped something small and furry into the underground cage.

"But, Iron Hans, please—" cried the voices, but they were silenced by the heavy door slamming down upon them again.

Jill's fear was replaced with anger. She had to control herself to keep from running at Iron Hans and beating him with her fists. She knew it would be useless. Even if she had a sword, Iron Hans could snap it like a toothpick.

So she fumed as Iron Hans clomped and thumped toward the castle. Mary rushed over to the cage door. "It's too heavy to move. The best we can do is mark the spot so we can find it later," said Mary as she removed her black bonnet and tied it to the branch of a nearby tree.

"Mary, this monster must be stopped!" Jill shouted with exasperation.

"Then we shall stop him," agreed Mary.

Jill said nothing, which at first made Mary think that she had calmed down. But Jill kept on saying nothing, and not moving or blinking either. Jill just stared with a glazed look on her face. It was yet another trance.

But because Jill still had the plight of the poor elves and hunters fresh in her memory, she felt less controlled this time. Her feelings of anger toward Iron Hans bubbled up like sour gas. Jill still saw the images of the prince, but that's all they were—images with no power.

As usual, the image shifted from the prince to the majestic castle, beautifully adorned with lights. This time, Jill was finally able to read the whole sign above the drawbridge.

shElves of Splendor, Aisles of Bliss
We Have the spRite Stuff
When Only the Best Will Do
Bring All Your Gold, Bring All Your Jewels
Or You Won't Have Enough Stuff
To Trade for a Kiss
By a Prince Who Will Marry You

Still in the trance, she could see the drawbridge lowering. Inside the castle there was a shop full of dresses and shoes and perfumes and makeup. Everything looked dazzling. Everything looked very expensive. As Jill watched the image flicker before her, she felt the urge to run home and find every piece of gold she could lay her hands on. She felt the desire to steal Jack's royal crown and bring it to this castle shop to trade. But in the corner of her mind, she remembered all the sad elves bent over their work, sweating as they sewed and stitched for hours upon hours, and the urge passed.

"Jill, snap out of it," Mary implored, gently shaking Jill out of the trance.

Jill's eyes focused on Mary and then she smiled. "It's okay, Mary, I'm not under its control anymore. I can resist it all by myself. And I know what Iron Hans intends to do."

Jill and Mary hiked back to the abandoned cottage where F.G. awaited them. For the rest of the day and late into the night, they tried to think of a way to defeat Iron Hans.

So a plan was made, and it was a good plan as far as plans go. That is, if everything had gone according to plan.

That evening Mary rode into the forest with a horse and cart that she had borrowed from the cobbler. In order to rescue the hunters, she intended to tie ropes from the cart to the cage door so the horse could pull it open.

In the meantime, Jill and Fairy Godmother went to pick up Cinderella at her stepmother's cottage and take her to the ball. When they reached the cottage, they found Cinderella washing dishes by an open window. But she wasn't alone.

"Don't forget to clean the root cellar while we're gone, do you hear me?" said a very unpleasant voice.

"Yes, Stepmother," replied Cinderella dismally.

"And clean the roots while you're at it!"

"Yes, Stepmother."

"I want my turnips sparkling, do you hear me? Sparkling!"

"Bye-bye, Cinderella!" squeaked another unpleasant voice. "While you're scrubbing tubers, I'll be saying 'I do' to my new fiancé!"

"Dream on!" shouted yet another unpleasant voice. "Prince Charming will be mine, sister!"

"Both of you, zip it! If we don't leave now, we'll miss out on the best stuff. I scrounged up all the gold we have, so each of you grab a sack of loot and let's go shopping!"

The front door squeaked open, allowing Jill a chance to spy Cinderella's stepfamily. They looked as unpleasant as they sounded. They had scrawny necks and hunched shoulders, and they clutched their sacks of gold with clawlike hands. They looked like of a flock of vultures as they plodded up the road toward the castle.

"Did you steal them?" asked Jill when Cinderella came out of the cottage.

"It wasn't easy, but here they are," replied Cinderella.

She pulled out two gold-embossed invitations from her apron pocket and then the three of them—Jill, Cinderella and Fairy Godmother—headed off to the ball. The road soon filled with more and more women going in the same direction, all of them carrying sacks stuffed with gold.

At Prince Charming's castle, the crowd funneled into a single line to cross the drawbridge. Jill, who had seen a very different castle the day before, gasped at the splendid sight before her. The scaffolding and long sheets of cloth were gone. What was revealed was a beautiful gleaming castle outlined in thousands of sparkling lights. This was the castle of Jill's trances, complete with the large sign over the drawbridge, enticing everyone to buy expensive clothes in order to attract the prince.

Up ahead in the line, the castle butler and Cinderella's stepsisters were arguing loudly.

"Ladies, if you do not possess invitations, then you most assuredly will *not* be attending this ball," said the butler sternly.

"We *have* invitations!" squawked the stepsisters in protest. "But we lost them!"

"How convenient," grimaced the butler.

"Mother, say something!" the sisters implored.

Cinderella's stepmother said nothing. She merely grabbed both sacks of gold from her daughters. "There's no use wasting these. I'll just buy myself more clothes. Don't wait up for Mommy, girls."

The two sisters were so stunned and upset, they didn't even notice Cinderella as they turned back toward their cottage in tears.

With the sisters out of the way, Jill and Cinderella planned to use their invitations to get into the ball while Fairy Godmother, using the only magic she could still rely upon, would make herself small enough to fit in Jill's pocket. Once inside, Fairy Godmother would shut off the Brain-Hypnotizing Machine and Jill would rescue Prince Charming's parents and the elf leader from the dungeon.

"Time to put this plan in action," said Jill.

The three of them moved off the road into the woods. Fairy Godmother scrunched up her face and grunted with the effort of making herself small. But nothing happened.

"We're too close to the castle," she explained. "It's messing up my magic."

"Try again," encouraged Jill.

Fairy Godmother scrunched up her face, and this time there was a *poof!* followed by a puff of smoke. However, it wasn't Fairy Godmother who had changed. It was

Jill. Fairy Godmother had turned Jill into another Prince Charming.

"This is just great," said Jill, in a much lower voice, and not really meaning it.

"Not to worry," said Fairy Godmother nervously. "I can fix that."

She made another attempt, and another, and several more after that. But sadly, nothing changed. Suffice it to say, their plan had a slight kink in it.

"What are we going to do now?" whispered Fairy Godmother and Cinderella frantically.

"Everyone calm down," said Jill, who now stood taller than her companions. "I'm thinking." Jill stroked her very square jaw and discovered beard stubble. "Ewww!"

"Look," said Jill finally, "we can still get into the castle. Since I look like Prince Charming, I don't need an invitation, so you can have mine." She handed her invitation to Fairy Godmother.

"But you need to hide those wings," Jill said as she removed her jacket and put it over Fairy Godmother's shoulders.

Then the three of them—Cinderella, Fairy Godmother and the fake Prince Charming—walked out of the woods, across the moat and up to the castle door.

"Prince Charming," exclaimed the bewildered butler, "what are you doing outside?"

"I needed to stretch my legs," replied Jill, thinking quickly, "and then I came upon this poor lady who was shivering in the evening air. So I offered her my coat for warmth. Now, step aside please."

"Yes, Your Majesty," bowed the butler, still looking confused. Before he could say another thing, Cinderella thrust two invitations into his hand, and then they all headed straight into the castle.

The whole main floor of the castle had been turned into a giant store. There were racks of dresses and rows of shoes and shelves full of hats and purses and gloves. It was all neatly organized, or at least it would have been if all the women of Grimm hadn't gone berserk.

"Give me that! I found them first!"

"Take a hike! Those are mine!"

"Lady, how would you like one of these shoes stuffed up your nose?"

The castle shop was in chaos. Women were everywhere, bustling and grabbing, fighting over dressing rooms, and demanding service. Exhausted elves scurried about trying to find proper sizes and quickly altering dresses to suit the women's tastes.

Jill didn't want to take a chance that someone might notice her. She ducked behind a tall shelf. Cinderella and Fairy Godmother squeezed in beside her.

"They're spending their gold like crazy," observed Fairy Godmother.

At the back of the room was the cashiers' counter. Women who had found what they wanted were handing over all their valuables. The elves then dumped all of it into wheelbarrows. Jill could see mounds of gold growing higher and higher with every purchase.

"How much for this outfit?" asked Cinderella's stepmother, all decked out in an outrageous gown, elbow-length gloves and shoes with dangerously tall thin heels.

"How much did you bring?" asked the elf on the other side of the counter.

"Three bags of gold."

"Lucky for you, that is exactly what your outfit costs."

At the back of the room, a red velvet curtain hung from ceiling to floor. Jill could see a huge hairy hand push the curtain far enough aside to allow a pair of glowing green eyes to peer into the shop.

"Iron Hans," Jill whispered, moving farther back behind the shelf. "We need to get to work. Cinderella, could you distract everyone so that Fairy Godmother and I can sneak out of here?"

Cinderella nodded confidently. "I think I can handle that."

Sweet polite Cinderella marched straight into the middle of the shop and climbed on top of a table. Then she took a deep breath and bellowed at the top of her lungs, "IF I DON'T GET SOME SERVICE IN THREE SECONDS, I'M GOING TO DO SOME SERIOUS DAMAGE!!!"

It took three seconds for thirteen elves to rush to Cinderella's assistance. And during those three seconds, the whole shop became completely quiet as every head turned in her direction. Jill and Fairy Godmother could have left the room hopping on pogo sticks without anyone noticing.

They ducked out into a hallway.

"The Brain-Hypnotizing Machine is that way," said Jill, pointing to the passage before them.

"Then that is where I will—Uh-oh!" exclaimed Fairy Godmother.

"Uh-oh?" asked Jill. "What do you mean—'Uh-oh'?"

Spurred into action, Fairy Godmother managed to use her basic fairy magic to make herself two inches tall. Then she ran down the hallway on her tiny fairy legs. A second later the shadow of Iron Hans loomed over Jill.

"Uh-oh," echoed Jill, who barely got the words out before Iron Hans grabbed her by the throat with one hand and lifted her way up in the air.

"What are you doing out of your room so soon?" demanded Iron Hans, who thought he was choking Prince Charming.

"I...I thought...I would meet all the

ladies? You know, do a little mingling," Jill gasped through his tight grip.

Iron Hans let Jill dangle in the air for a few moments, studying her closely. "You'd better not play tricks with me, Prince, or I'll press this button so fast your parents will look like coleslaw."

Iron Hans held a small black box in his other hand. It had a red button in the middle. He brought it up close to Jill, squinting his repulsive green eyes and smirking hideously.

"No tricks, Iron Hans, honest," Jill lied. "Please don't hurt his...my parents. They haven't done anything."

Iron Hans opened his grip, allowing Jill to fall hard to the floor. While she rubbed her sore neck, Iron Hans dragged her up by her shirt collar and shoved her toward two large wooden doors. He opened them wide. Jill was overcome by the dazzling sound of waltz music. This was the castle ballroom, and it was quickly filling up with more and more women.

"All right, Prince," snarled Iron Hans as

he pushed Jill into the ballroom. "Go and mingle."

The door slammed behind her, drawing the attention of all the ladies in the room. There were hundreds of them, all dressed up. Young women, older women, witches and stepmothers, little girls and dear old grannies. They stared at Jill in utter fascination. They were drawn to her like moths to a flame. She was Prince Charming, as far as they could tell. She was the prince of their trances, more valuable than gold.

Jill smiled meekly. I really need to get away from them, she thought.

Jill stood up straight and tried to imagine how it felt to be Prince Charming. She thrust her shoulders out and with a steady confident gaze, walked through the crowd. The women parted respectfully, each hoping that the prince would ask her to dance.

But Jill didn't say a word. She continued across the floor toward the set of glass doors leading outside to a terrace.

By the time the women figured out what had happened, Jill had closed the doors behind her.

Thick vines crept up the castle walls, and Jill could make out a turret at the very top. There was a light shining through its windows. She was sure it was the prince's room.

Without a second to spare, Jill began climbing up the ivy.

For the second time since arriving in Grimm, Jill found herself climbing a steep stone wall high above the ground. But this time she was doing it in another person's body—a bigger, bulkier body.

Once Jill reached the turret at the very top, she had a full view of the forest at the back of the castle, but could see no sign of Mary and the rescued hunters. However, she spied a horse and cart parked beside the moat. There was a wooden chute stretched across the moat, coming from one of the castle's lower windows. Even from high up, it was easy to tell what was sliding down that chute—it was all the gold the women had brought. Iron Hans was loading his loot in preparation for his escape.

Jill would have loved to frighten the horse away and leave Iron Hans without any gold. But first things first, Jill told herself as she climbed into Prince Charming's bedroom.

"Hello, Prince Charming," she said, "and no, you haven't gone crazy," she added when she saw the expression on his face.

Prince Charming was not entirely convinced. He was, after all, staring at a person that looked and sounded exactly like himself. But Jill quickly explained the mix-up and reassured him that she was ready to rescue his parents.

"Jill, are you sure you can do it? From what I hear, Iron Hans has made it next to impossible to escape the dungeon."

"You can trust me as you can trust yourself, I guess," replied Jill.

Jill and Prince Charming left his bedroom and snuck down the many staircases toward the main floor of the castle. They made absolutely sure that no one spotted them.

"Here's where we part company," whispered Prince Charming, heading toward the ballroom. "The dungeon is down there."

He pointed to one final staircase that sank below the floor. Jill couldn't see anything but shadows beyond the first few stony steps.

"Remember, you must hold off choosing Cinderella as your bride for as long as you can," Jill insisted. "I'll give you a signal when everyone is safe. Until then, you'll have to keep all the women occupied, and Iron Hans as well. He's lurking about the hallways. Good luck."

Prince Charming watched Jill descend into the gloomy darkness below. "Good luck to you too," he called out after her.

As a rule, dungeons tend to be damp dark cells with thick iron doors locked by heavy chains. They may also contain the odd bit of furniture like a bed or leg irons.

To Jill's surprise, this was not what she found. This dungeon was nothing more than an open room at the end of a long stone corridor. Prince Charming's parents and the elf leader were just sitting in the room, having a pleasant chat.

"Hello, son," said Prince Charming's mother. She waved pleasantly in Jill's direction.

"We've been having a most interesting conversation with Karl," added Prince Charming's father. "It seems that most of the goods sold in the shops in Grimm are actually made by elves. They get paid less than nothing for their efforts. Imagine that!"

The wizened old elf leader said nothing at first, but Jill was pretty sure that he rolled his eyes. Then he stood up and turned toward Jill. "Has Iron Hans finally left the castle, Prince Charming?" he asked.

Jill decided not to tell any of them who she really was. It might have set them off in a panic.

"Not yet, sir," replied Jill. "I came here to rescue you, but...I really don't see what's keeping you from walking out."

From what Jill could see, there was nothing between her and the three prisoners except about one hundred steps along a stone floor.

"I will give you the same demonstration that Iron Hans gave us," said Karl.

The white-bearded elf walked over to a table in the far corner of the room and picked up a honeydew melon from a fruit dish. Then he returned to the front of the room and proceeded to bowl the melon down the hallway toward Jill. The melon didn't get more than two feet before it was sliced by a very large knife that came out of a fissure in the wall. Then another blade came down from the ceiling, followed by another blade shooting out of the floor. As the melon continued to roll along, it was gashed and hacked by more and more steel blades. By the time the honeydew stopped at Jill's feet, it had been sliced into fifty thin pieces.

"Ah," said Jill. But there was something else. Something about how the blades cut the melon caught Jill's attention. She just couldn't put her finger on it.

"Isn't it amazing?" exclaimed Prince Charming's father. "Quite deadly, don't you think? And it was all made by elves, I am told. They really are good with their hands."

This time both Jill *and* Karl rolled their eyes.

"Iron Hans has a hundred more sharp blades over here," sighed Karl, indicating their cell. "He could chop us into bits whenever he wanted. All he needs to do is press a button on the box he keeps in his pocket."

"I've seen that box," nodded Jill, remembering Iron Hans's grip on her throat. "Is there no way to turn this killing machine off?"

"Yes, there is a switch. Unfortunately, it is exactly halfway between you and us. Plenty of blades, either way."

"The elves who made this were very clever," conceded Jill.

"Yes," agreed Karl. "Elves hate to do shoddy work. There is an old elf saying, 'Even bad music can be saved by good dancing.'"

"That's it!" yelled Jill. "Dancing! I knew there was something familiar about those blades! Bowl another melon toward me."

"But son," scolded Prince Charming's mother, "you haven't even eaten the first one. What does Mother always say about wasting food?"

Jill had no time to roll her eyes. She studied the second honeydew as it made its gruesome journey through the knives. "Chop. Chop. Cut from the right. Then stop. Fox-trot!" she yelled. "Roll another one!"

Karl picked up a third melon and sent it toward Jill.

"Bend knees. Slice. Slice. Jab from the left. Slide together. Tango!" she laughed out loud. "One more!"

"It will have to be," said Karl, "since this is the last melon."

Jill concentrated hard on the fourth and final melon. "Thrust from the right. Backward rock. Cut forward. Left stab. Stab again. Bend forward. Slice. Thrust from the right. Cha-cha-cha!"

Prince Charming's parents and the elf leader were staring at Jill with expressions of grave concern. They clearly had no idea what she was babbling about. But Jill knew exactly what she was doing. Allow *her* to explain.

"Who would ever have thought that something useful would come out of those stupid ballroom dance lessons? The knives are coming out of the walls in the same step pattern as three dances: the fox-trot, the tango and the cha-cha. All I need to do is walk across the floor doing those three dances and I should arrive at the on/off switch in one piece."

"Well done!" shouted Karl.

"That's my boy!" seconded Prince Charming's father.

"What do you mean by 'stupid dance lessons'?" asked Prince Charming's mother in a very hurt voice. Apparently Mother Goose wasn't the only royal mother who insisted on dance lessons.

Jill took a deep breath. She went over all the dance moves in her head, and when she felt she was ready, she took her first step. ZING! SLICE! JAB! CUT! SLASH! SLICE! JAB! CUT! SLASH! It was breathtaking. Jill moved perfectly to the rhythm of the dozens of blades trying to get her, but she always stayed out of their reach. She bent forward when she was supposed to bend forward. She bent backward when she was supposed to bend back. She stepped right. She stepped left. She paused when a pause was required. It would have been enough to simply avoid getting chopped up, but Jill did even more. She made it look beautiful. Had there been official judges in that dungeon, she would have scored a perfect ten.

Jill reached the midpoint of the corridor. Sure enough, there was a gap between two stones and a red light flashing from within it. She reached in and pressed a button and the light turned green. The dungeon was no longer deadly.

"Let's get you out of here," said Jill, ushering everyone down the hallway toward the stairs.

By the time Jill, Karl and Prince
Charming's parents had climbed up
from the dungeon, Fairy Godmother,
now back to her normal size, had also
returned. Everyone met in the castle's
main hallway.

"Fairy Godmother!" Jill exclaimed. "Did
you shut off the machine?"

"We shall soon find out."

With a nod of her head, Fairy Godmother
made a *poof!* followed by a puff of smoke.
When it cleared, Jill had turned back into
her usual Jill self.

"I guess I did," Fairy Godmother said
with a satisfied smile.

But from Prince Charming's parents' point of view, Fairy Godmother had just turned their eighteen-year-old son into an eleven-year-old girl. Prince Charming's father fainted. Prince Charming's mother made a mental note to redecorate Prince Charming's bedroom. Then she too fainted.

"We have to stop Iron Hans before he makes his escape!" Jill beseeched Fairy Godmother.

She ran down the hall with Fairy Godmother close behind. When Jill came around the last corner, she discovered Iron Hans beside a large open window. He was shoveling gold out of the final wheelbarrow and onto the chute that led across the moat to the horse and cart.

"Iron Hans, you are taking what does not belong to you!" Jill yelled.

Caught by surprise, Iron Hans turned to face his accuser. However, when he saw it was just a skinny girl, he growled with annoyance. "Let me guess, you must be Princess Jill. I thought my

Brain-Hypnotizing Machine would have taken care of you."

"I order you to stop what you are doing!" demanded Jill.

Iron Hans bellowed with laughter. "Or what? Whatever are *you* going to do to *me*?"

Just then Fairy Godmother came around the corner. She cast a spell that made the heavy wheelbarrow crash into the back of Iron Hans's knees, causing him to fall into it. "Well, we can do *that* for a start, Iron Hans," she said threateningly. "And then I can use a spell that was especially created for you and no one else."

Iron Hans didn't look so confident anymore. He struggled to get back onto his feet as fast as he could. But it wasn't fast enough to escape Fairy Godmother's spell.

"Where I see your rusted metal,
I'll wilt you like a flower petal.
And where I see such evil plans,
I'll put an end to Iron Hans!"

As she spoke, a bolt of lightning came blasting out of Fairy Godmother's fingertips. It hit directly where Iron Hans's heart would be, assuming he actually had one. It caused sparks to fly in all directions. It left thick black smoke billowing up into the air. It was quite dramatic in every way, but it didn't seem to do any harm to Iron Hans, leaving both him and Fairy Godmother very surprised.

"I don't understand," said Fairy Godmother. "It should have worked."

"The spell might have worked on Iron Hans," said a voice coming from somewhere inside Iron Hans, "but it won't work on us."

Iron Hans's chest suddenly opened up, revealing two elves strapped inside his body.

They were clutching levers that made the arms and legs and head move.

Jill gasped. Beneath the jungle of beastly hair was not a layer of rust-colored skin. Iron Hans was actually covered in small sheets of rusty metal held together by

rivets. Iron Hans was made of iron. No wonder he was so strong, Jill thought.

"You mean that all along, it was just two greedy and mean-spirited elves in a machine causing all the problems in Grimm?" she asked.

"Just?" yelled one of the angry elves. "*Just* two elves? These two elves have pulled off the greatest crime in Grimm! Right, Dickey?"

"You said it, Taters!" growled the other elf.

And in a blink, the two elves scurried from their Iron Hans machine and dived out the window. By the time Jill reached the window, they had already slid down the chute and onto the front of the cart. Dickey gave the reins of the horse a strong shake, and in an instant, they were off at a fast clip.

Jill leaned out the window and moaned, "Oh, no! They got away with all the gold."

From across the moat, shadows came out of the forest, and soon after, Jill could make out Mary and the four missing hunters. And behind them there was something else. It was a horse and cart, and it too was filled with gold.

"You're right, Princess Jill," Mary called out. "They did escape. But they didn't get away with the gold. They actually got away with a bunch of useless rocks painted to look like gold. We traded carts two minutes ago."

Jill felt amazingly better after hearing that. She smiled at Mary. "Well done. I wish I could see their faces when they discover that this whole evil plan was a waste of time."

"Not a complete waste for Prince Charming and Cinderella," Mary pointed out.

"That's right! I nearly forgot! I have to let Prince Charming know that his parents and the elf leader are safe."

Jill pulled her head back inside the window and dashed over to the ball-room, where she found Prince Charming gallantly dancing with one woman after another. Single-handedly, he was trying to keep all of them amused and happy. Well, perhaps not everyone. Since the Brain-Hypnotizing Machine had been destroyed, the women were no longer under its control, and many were wondering what on earth was going on.

Jill made her way toward the prince.

"Hello, Prince Charming. Your parents and the elf leader are now safe. The missing hunters have been rescued. The women of Grimm are no longer in a trance."

"That's wonderful! You have been a true hero to our land. The people of Grimm will always be grateful to you," promised Prince Charming as he bowed to her graciously.

The ballroom doors swung open and Karl entered with all the happy elves around him. But when Prince Charming saw his parents being led inside by Fairy Godmother, he said to Jill, "There is one more thing I should do before this evening comes to an end."

He went over to his parents, took them by their hands and walked into the middle of the room. In a frank and forthright voice, Prince Charming addressed everyone. "Dear women of Grimm, a terrible trick has been played upon you, and it was done for no other reason than to separate you from your money."

With Jill and Fairy Godmother's help, he explained how the terrible events had unfolded.

"Finally, I wish to say that even though Iron Hans isn't here to force me to marry, there really is someone whom I wish to marry. Her name is Cinderella. We have known each other for quite some time, and I care for her deeply."

All heads turned toward Cinderella, who was standing all alone beside a tall vase of flowers. She was still dressed in the same ragged clothes she always wore. She was not adorned with perfume or makeup or jewels. No magic had brought her to the castle—just her love for the prince, and that was more than enough.

"Here comes the mushy stuff," sighed Jill. And sure enough, it did. Jill tried her best not to grimace.

The celebration continued through the night. Jill, Mary and Fairy Godmother stood outside on the ballroom terrace and watched the sun rise. It streaked the soft blue sky with orange-pink stripes. The flowers yawned awake and the sparrows chirped as if the land of Grimm was reborn into something, well, less grim. It was a lovely day.

Fairy Godmother took Jill's hands into her own and looked warmly into Jill's eyes. "You exceeded my expectations, Jill. You showed great bravery and leadership, but you showed compassion as well. I have no doubt that we will be hearing more about you in the future. Let us consider ourselves friends."

Fairy Godmother leaned over and kissed Jill on the forehead.

"We should get going," said Mary. "We still have a couple of days of travel before us."

"Not to worry," said Fairy Godmother. "My magic should be able to get you to the border of our two lands. That will cut your trip in half."

And then, in the time it takes to go *poof!* Jill and Mary found themselves sitting on their horses at the edge of Grimm's dark forest. The kingdom of Mother Goose stood before them, and Mary's cottage was close by.

"You know, Mary," Jill said hesitantly, "you don't have to go right home. You could come and spend a few days at the castle. I could show you around."

"No, you couldn't."

Jill was taken aback. Her offer was heartfelt. Then Jill saw that Mary was grinning. "Yes, I could," said Jill, playing along.

"No, you couldn't," giggled Mary. But she turned her horse away from her home and headed toward Mother Goose's castle.

Jill gazed out at the Mother Goose countryside and smiled.

"Home sweet home," she whispered under her breath. And she really meant it too.

Read the first book about
King Jack and Princess Jill.

In *Things are Looking Up, Jack*, all is not right in the land of Mother Goose. People and things keep falling down, and it is not just a coincidence. There is trouble afoot. It is up to King Jack and his sister Princess Jill to get to the bottom of this mystery.

"Bar-el's story is a riveting and often hilarious romp through an imaginative landscape that will keep readers guessing about the final outcome".

—*Canadian Literature*

photo credit: Dominique Bréchault

When not hitching a ride on a broomstick with a passing witch or teaching marmots to play guitar, **Dan Bar-el** is an early childhood educator, a writer, a storyteller and a very funny guy. *Things are Looking Up, Jack*, his first book about hapless King Jack and reckless Princess Jill, was published by Orca in 2003. His picturebook *Alphabetter* is due out from Orca in fall 2006. Dan lives in Vancouver, British Columbia.

Orca Young Readers

Jo's Journey
Jo's Triumph
Five Stars for Emily
Just Call Me Joe

Nikki Tate
Nikki Tate
Kathleen Cook Waldron
Frieda Wishinsky

Orca Young Readers Series

Max and Ellie series by Becky Citra
Ellie's New Home, The Freezing Moon,
Danger at the Landings, Runaway,
Strawberry Moon

TJ series by Hazel Hutchins
TJ and the Cats, TJ and the Haunted House,
TJ and the Rockets, TJ and the Sports Fanatic

Basketball series by Eric Walters
Three on Three, Full Court Press, Hoop Crazy!
Long Shot, Road Trip, Off Season, Underdog,
Triple Threat

Kaylee and Sausage series by Anita Daher
Flight from Big Tangle and
Flight from Bear Canyon